George and the Dragon

by Anne Adeney and Peter Kavanagh

FRANKLIN WATTS
LONDON•SYDNEY

George and the Dragon

First published in 2006 by
Franklin Watts
338 Euston Road
London
NW1 3BH

Franklin Watts Australia
Level 17/207 Kent Street
Sydney
NSW 2000

A CIP catalogue record for this book is available
from the British Library.

ISBN 978 0 7496 6691 0

Series Editor: Jackie Hamley
Series Advisor: Dr Barrie Wade
Series Designer: Peter Scoulding

Printed in China

Franklin Watts is a division of
Hachette Children's Books,
an Hachette Livre UK company.

For Harvey and Megan,
and their great imaginations – P.K.

George was a soldier, strong and brave. He rode a huge horse called Bayard.

One day he saw the King and all his people weeping and wailing. "What's wrong?" asked George.

"The dragon is going to eat my daughter!" the King cried.

"Our only water comes from
a spring, which is guarded by
a fierce dragon.

"He won't let us have any water unless we feed him every day. He's already gobbled up all our sheep and goats."

"Now he demands a young girl
to eat every day," said the King.

"We had a lottery to see who would
be eaten first and the Princess lost!"

"Please fight that wicked dragon," begged the King. "Otherwise the Princess and all our young girls will die!"

"I will fight this greedy monster,"
said brave George. He put on his
armour and picked up his weapons.

13

George rode Bayard to the
spring just below the town.

The townspeople watched
from a safe distance.

The foulest odour that George had
ever smelt filled the air. Suddenly
there was a roar like thunder as
the dragon soared down upon
him. Its vast wings blocked
out the sun.

A great burst of flame shot from the dragon's mouth. Bayard's tail was sizzled like a sausage.

George aimed his lance at the
dragon's body and charged.

But the dragon's shimmering scales
were so hard that George's lance
crumbled into a thousand pieces.

He was thrown to the ground and Bayard raced for the safety of the town. George rolled under a tree and drew his sword.

Another burst of flames set the tree
ablaze and the heat cracked the
soldier's armour wide open.

Without any armour, George hid
amongst the rocks. The dragon
roared as it lost sight of its prey.

It lifted its wings to soar into the sky and search for George.

Brave George leapt out and thrust his sword under the dragon's wing.

There were no scales to protect the dragon here and the blade went straight into its heart

Dark blood burst forth and
stained the ground.

The dragon was dead and the
Princess was saved!

The people of the town rejoiced
and the King gave George a huge
bag of gold as a reward.

George used it to buy more sheep and goats for the people of the town. Then he went quietly on his way.

Hopscotch has been specially designed to fit the requirements of the National Literacy Strategy. It offers real books by top authors and illustrators for children developing their reading skills. There are 49 Hopscotch stories to choose from:

Marvin, the Blue Pig
ISBN 978 0 7496 4619 6

Plip and Plop
ISBN 978 0 7496 4620 2

The Queen's Dragon
ISBN 978 0 7496 4618 9

Flora McQuack
ISBN 978 0 7496 4621 9

Willie the Whale
ISBN 978 0 7496 4623 3

Naughty Nancy
ISBN 978 0 7496 4622 6

Run!
ISBN 978 0 7496 4705 6

The Playground Snake
ISBN 978 0 7496 4706 3

"Sausages!"
ISBN 978 0 7496 4707 0

Bear in Town
ISBN 978 0 7496 5875 5

Pippin's Big Jump
ISBN 978 0 7496 4710 0

Whose Birthday Is It?
ISBN 978 0 7496 4709 4

The Princess and the Frog
ISBN 978 0 7496 5129 9

Flynn Flies High
ISBN 978 0 7496 5130 5

Clever Cat
ISBN 978 0 7496 5131 2

Moo!
ISBN 978 0 7496 5332 3

Izzie's Idea
ISBN 978 0 7496 5334 7

Roly-poly Rice Ball
ISBN 978 0 7496 5333 0

I Can't Stand It!
ISBN 978 0 7496 5765 9

Cockerel's Big Egg
ISBN 978 0 7496 5767 3

How to Teach a Dragon Manners
ISBN 978 0 7496 5873 1

The Truth about those Billy Goats
ISBN 978 0 7496 5766 6

Marlowe's Mum and the Tree House
ISBN 978 0 7496 5874 8

The Truth about Hansel and Gretel
ISBN 978 0 7496 4708 7

The Best Den Ever
ISBN 978 0 7496 5876 2

ADVENTURE STORIES

Aladdin and the Lamp
ISBN 978 0 7496 6692 7

Blackbeard the Pirate
ISBN 978 0 7496 6690 3

George and the Dragon
ISBN 978 0 7496 6691 0

Jack the Giant-Killer
ISBN 978 0 7496 6693 4

TALES OF KING ARTHUR

1. The Sword in the Stone
ISBN 978 0 7496 6694 1

2. Arthur the King
ISBN 978 0 7496 6695 8

3. The Round Table
ISBN 978 0 7496 6697 2

4. Sir Lancelot and the Ice Castle
ISBN 978 0 7496 6698 9

TALES OF ROBIN HOOD

Robin and the Knight
ISBN 978 0 7496 6699 6

Robin and the Monk
ISBN 978 0 7496 6700 9

Robin and the Silver Arrow
ISBN 978 0 7496 6703 0

Robin and the Friar
ISBN 978 0 7496 6702 3

The Emperor's New Clothes
ISBN 978 0 7496 7081 2

Cinderella
ISBN 978 0 7496 7017 5

Snow White
ISBN 978 0 7496 7076 8

Jack and the Beanstalk
ISBN 978 0 7496

The Three Billy Goats Gruff
ISBN 978 0 7496

of London
ISBN 978 0 7496 7079 5 *
ISBN 978 0 7496 7410 6

Pocahontas the Peacemaker
ISBN 978 0 7496 7080 1 *
ISBN 978 0 7496 7411 3

Grandma's Seaside Bloomers
ISBN 978 0 7496 7081 8 *
ISBN 978 0 7496 7412 0

Hoorah for Mary Seacole
ISBN 978 0 7496 7082 5 *
ISBN 978 0 7496 7413 7

Remember the 5th of November
ISBN 978 0 7496 7083 2 *
ISBN 978 0 7496 7414 4

Tutankhamun and the Golden Chariot
ISBN 978 0 7496 7084 9 *
ISBN 978 0 7496 7415 1

* hardback